Sissy Dreams:
Collection 12

Sissy Dreams:
Collection 12

Story Copyrights © Paul Zante 2019
Paperback version © Paul Zante 2021

ISBN: 9798747528673

Author's note: All characters portrayed are over 18 years old.

Contents

One of the girls

I could tell my room-mates, Kayla and Claire, were home by the amount of giggling and shushing going on outside the front door. I knew they weren't shushing each other so as not to disturb me, but the neighbours. The three of us shared an apartment and felt it best not to advertise our... living arrangements.

Should I open the front door? Or let them fumble around in their bags for the keys? Assuming of course that it was their keys they were fumbling around for...

I stood in my currently favourite dress undecided what to do. The tall mirror in the hallway told me my feminine figure looked gorgeous in the smooth satin I wore.

But then a particularly loud squeal-type giggle sounded (that I knew came from Kayla), deciding it for me and I quickly opened the door to the two girls. I almost burst out laughing at their wide-eyed surprise at seeing me like I was some sort of angry parent. Or maybe they just weren't expecting Cinderella to open it for them?

Thankfully Claire, possibly the less drunk of the two, grabbed Kayla and hurried her inside past me. I quickly shut and locked the door behind them, already imagining the pissy note from the apartment manager after our neighbours cornered him and had a 'talk'.

Now inside they collapsed against each other in a fit of giggles. Thankfully they still had their clothes on, although it seemed that a lot more skin was showing past a pair of miniskirts, Claire's white cropped blouse, and Kayla's glittery bandeau, than would normally be acceptable in polite society.

Only a short moment later their lips were stuck to each other's and they were vigorously making out. When their hands strayed to each other's miniskirt (Kayla in a lovely shiny hologram material that showed rainbows everywhere, and Claire in a tarty slit-sided leather one) I felt it best to leave them to it and clicked in my silver stilettos to the kitchen to get them some juice. They'd probably need the vitamins after their sweaty exertions at the club they'd come home from.

The sound of Kayla's mirror heels and Claire's shiny leather stiletto boots along the hallway told me they'd somehow managed to move into the lounge. So I placed the two frosting glasses on a small metal tray and, like the good sissy maid I was, went to serve my mistresses there.

The scent of their perfumes met me as I entered. Slouched on the sofa they were still engrossed in kissing each other, and didn't seem to hear my welcoming "Mistress Claire, Mistress Kayla," nor see the perfect curtseys I made for each of them while still holding the tray. I sighed inwardly at not being appreciated and placed the tray on the table set to one side of the sofa then went to stand waiting for instructions. In one of their brief kissing lulls Claire saw the drinks and she disentangled herself from Kayla, exclaiming, "Sissy! You're a lifesaver!"

It seemed I just had to wait a bit. "Thank you, Mistress."

I stood by waiting for more orders while Claire leant forwards (thereby giving me a good look at her cleavage down her cropped white blouse), picked up both glasses and handed one to Kayla.

They quickly drank some then sighed with relief at the cold tartness of the juice.

"Enjoyable evening, Mistresses?"

"Yes, thank you. Been busy with our laundry, Cinderella?" Claire said, her blue-shadowed eyes regarded me over the frosted top of her glass. Maybe the dress wasn't quite the right one to wear tonight? I didn't want them thinking they were in any way ugly.

"Yes, Mistress. It's all done and put away."

"Not before enjoying herself with our panties, I'll bet," whispered Kayla, failing miserably to hide her voice behind her own glass.

I felt my cheeks heat up and quickly decided to quickly change the topic. "Foot rubs, anyone?"

"Ooh, me first!" said Kayla, quickly kicking her mirror silver heels off.

Claire sighed at the lost opportunity and took another pull on her drink. I felt her eyes on me as my gown rustled as I knelt down in front of Kayla and placed her left foot on my satin-covered right thigh and slowly began massaging her foot. I noticed the red polish on her toenails needed a top-up. Something to do at our next girls night in pampering session.

"You're looking very pretty tonight, Sissy," Claire said while Kayla closed her eyes and moaned with pleasure beside her.

"Thank you, mistress."

"You've always wanted to be a beautiful princess?"

"Haven't we all?" I think what made me want to be Cinderella was the addition of the satin choker. So pretty and feminine.

"Is that a new lipstick?"

She'd always been the more observant one.

"Yes. I saw it in Glamour a while back. It came today and I just had to wear it. You think it suits me?"

Still looking at me Claire turned her head and stage-whispered, "You know Sissy's looking at your panties, Kayla?"

Kayla groaned and replied, "I don't care. Here," Still with her left foot on my thigh and a half-drunk glass of cold juice in her left hand she held the hem of her hologram skirt with her right and shuffled her ass forwards making her skirt lift up. Then moved her knees apart giving me an unobstructed look at her black panties.

"Kayla!" Claire exclaimed, feigning outraged shock.

"Don' care! This is so good!"

Claire rolled her eyes at Kayla's actions, then turned back to me. "I see you've also done something with your hair, Sissy."

She was right. I'd played around with my curling wand and now my long hair just cascaded in beautiful waves around the blue satin band that matched the gown. I was rather proud of what I'd accomplished.

Claire's calculating eyes took me in while she took another sip. Seemingly unconcerned I changed Kayla's feet over and elicited more groans from her as I started on her other foot.

"So, a new hairstyle, and new lipstick?"

"Yes, Mistress. I hope you both approve?"

"Would you be making yourself pretty for a reason, Sissy?"

I shrugged. "I like to look pretty and feminine, Mistress."

Claire took another sip to finish her drink then lifted her right leg and unzipped her knee-high boot. The sound sharp against Kayla's groans of pleasure. "It is a lovely lipstick shade, Sissy. But I think it needs to be tested out."

I looked up at her, puzzled. "Mistress?"

"Take these," she said, giving me her empty glass and indicating Kayla's. I took them and placed them as far away from us as I could reach on the floor.

She straightened her right leg and the unzipped long leather boot fell off it. Her naked foot found my face and she began rubbing her toes against my lips. I could smell her sweaty foot scent and saw that she, too, needed her nail polish touched up.

"How does that feel, Sissy?" she said, trying to worm her toes into my mouth.

I knew that if I said anything she'd stick them right in. But if I didn't open my mouth I'd be a bad sissy maid. But I also knew that she loved her toes and feet being licked and sucked. Maybe this would divert her from enquiring what I'd got up to with their used panties?

"It– ungh!" Her foot invaded my mouth preventing me from talking.

"Lick my toes," she ordered.

I ran my tongue over her toes, making them wet and slippery. How far would she force her foot into my mouth? Did she want me to take all her toes?

"Bitch," said Kayla, beside her. "Wish I'd thought of that."

"Worship my toes, Sissy. You snooze you lose, dear," she added in Kayla's direction.

"If you suck my toes I'll let you sniff my panties, Sissy. While I'm still wearing them."

Kayla was trying, and succeeding, in getting my attention. But Claire was having none of it.

"Between the toes, Sissy. I know how you love sniffing my shoes."

It seemed that they knew most of my fetishes.

As ordered I slid my warm, wet tongue between Claire's toes. She gave a satisfied groan and closed her eyes.

"Suck them," she whispered.

Slowly I began moving my head forwards and back, gently sucking her toes, my soft lips rubbing against them.

Excited feelings rushed down underneath my blue satin gown and my cock squeezed itself against the small pink chastity cage I wore. It was one of the conditions of my sharing an apartment with these two gorgeous girls. Also, no male clothes were permitted to be worn in the apartment. Strangely enough I had no argument with this stipulation.

She moved her left leg and reached down to unzip her other boot. Was I going to have to take both her feet in my mouth?

Her boot fell to the floor and she opened her eyes to watch me suck her toes and massage Kayla's foot.

"I know what you'd like, Sissy."

Was she going to show me her panties as well?

Slowly she stretched out her left leg so her toes found the smooth satin of my bodice. Slowly they rubbed the soft material. Her big toe moved down and dragged the front of my gown with it, slowly revealing the top of my pale blue satin corset. The tops of my growing breasts peeking over the top. Then it moved further down, over my stomach, sending thrills through me, until she lay it on top of the gown's satin skirt in my lap.

"Suck my big toe, Princess."

I released her right foot and leant down. Like it was a very short cock (rather like my own in its cage) I slowly licked and ran my soft lips up and down it. She closed her eyes in pleasure, and moved her right foot so her toes were underneath my gown and between my legs. Her left hand found its way to her black panties and she slowly began to rub herself through them.

At roughly the same time her foot found my matching pale blue satin panties that contained my clit-like pink chastity cage. She slowly began rubbing the sole of her foot against it in time with her own left hand against her panties.

Kayla looked on as her lover pleasured herself and decided to do the same. Her right hand delved underneath her own black panties and slowly began rubbing her sensitive lips, sighing at the waves of pleasure she felt.

My cage slowly got tighter against my trapped dick at the sight and smell of two hot lesbians masturbating. I wished I could lick and suck them to orgasm but I still had Claire's big toe in my mouth and Kayla's foot in my hands.

Claire then stopped rubbing my cage through the panties and I groaned as she moved it underneath to play with my balls through the blue satin.

It wasn't long before Kayla began pushing a wet finger up inside herself, her body shuddering with delight. She moved her other hand across to Claire's panties and slipped them underneath the wet material, making her lover groan as she began fingering her as well.

Claire took her right foot away from my mouth and moved her leg wide to give Kayla more space to get at her hot musky cunt. Her left foot moved a bit further between my stockinged legs and began rubbing the sensitive area between my balls and anus. I had to close my eyes as intense tingles rushed through me and my balls. How far would she go?

"Fuck me!" Kayla pleaded. "Fuck me with your new dildo!"

"Give it to me, slut!" ordered Claire.

Kayla obviously knew where it was as she quickly reached over the top of the sofa and brought back a blue rubber dildo with its straps hanging down.

"Sissy, put it on me."

"Mistress."

Regretfully I moved away from Claire's foot and took the strap-on away from Kayla. She took off her skirt and slid her panties off to let Claire get at her hot, musky cunt. She caught my eye and smiled as she played at sniffing and licking her warm, wet panties. Then put them to one side and turned to kneel on the sofa's edge, her hands on the top, and wiggled her bubbly ass in Claire's face.

"Hurry up, Sissy, I need to fuck this slut."

"Mistress."

I undid Claire's slit leather skirt, took it and her panties off and lay them on the sofa's armrest before strapping the blue dildo on her.

"Fuck me!" Kayla excitedly whispered, her sexy ass waving invitingly.

"Wet it, Princess."

Quickly I moved closer and licked the dildo from tip to base, getting it as wet as possible for Kayla. Although she seemed wet enough already.

This was normally the time for me to leave and let them get on with it, while I did something else around the apartment. Like cleaning or something. But this evening took a different turn.

"You wanna help me fuck a slut, Princess?"

"Sorry?"

"Turn around and get your face between her legs. This slut needs to be fucked hard."

She wanted me to participate?

"Mistress!" I quickly slid my ass up against the base of the sofa, the satin of my dress rustling, and got my mouth into position, less than an inch away from Kayla's clit, ready to lick it when Claire told me to.

Kayla's gorgeous body hung above me, her breasts quivering with anticipation. Could she feel my hot breath on her sensitive lips?

I felt Claire's feet move so that she stood either side of my pale blue satin Cinderella gown. Kayla looked behind her and moaned at the sight of Claire moving ever so closer with her dildo.

"Does the slut want this?" Claire crooned. I saw her hand slowly move the tip of the blue dildo up and down, barely touching Kayla's sensitive lips.

"Please!" Kayla moaned, pushing her ass back, trying to get the dildo into her wet hole.

"What are you?" Claire whispered.

"A slut!"

"What do you want?"

Kayla moaned with frustration. "To be fucked! Fuck me!"

The dildo tip slowly pushed into Kayla's cunt and stopped.

Kayla gasped, her body quivering.

"Does slut want more?"

"Yes!"

"Suck the slut, Princess."

My tongue sprang into action, licking and slurping at Kayla's pussy, greedily tasting her hot juice.

Kayla held her breath as the feeling overwhelmed her. Then gasped "ohgodohgodohgod" as Claire pushed the blue dildo further into her wet cunt.

My tongue slipped around and flicked her hard swollen clit as Claire started to pump the dildo in and out of Kayla's cunt, its fake balls bouncing off my chin.

I saw Kayla's body tremble and her muscles tighten up then release as orgasms built up and then exploded within her. Her breathing quickened until she was gasping with each thrust and suck I gave her clit.

She gave a deep "Ohhh," and I felt Claire move away.

"Suck it, Princess!"

I opened my mouth and Claire filled it with the warm, wet dildo. I eagerly sucked it, tasting Kayla's juice, and feeling it rub against my tongue and soft lips as Claire thrust it in and out. A mix of Kayla's pussy juice and my saliva ran down my chin.

"More!" Kayla pleaded.

Claire took the dildo out of my mouth and then Kayla squealed as she suddenly thrust it balls-deep into her hot, wet cunt.

I moved to continue licking Kayla as Claire thrust harder and harder.

Kayla could barely draw a breath with all the orgasms exploding within her body. I saw her body tense even more and gasp for breath as a huge orgasm began to build.

It only took a few more thrusts before she groaned aloud, her whole body rigid as the orgasm smashed into her, and then she collapsed onto the sofa. Slowly her rapid breathing went back to normal.

I thought that was it until Claire asked, "Want to be fucked?"

Hadn't she already fucked Kayla? Not entirely sure what she meant or who she was talking to, I looked up at her.

Her eyes burned into mine. "Want me to fuck you like a horny slut, Princess?"

She'd never offered to do this to me before.

"Like I did with this hot piece of ass?" she indicated the recovering Kayla.

"Hey, Princess," Kayla whispered. I looked up at her over her gorgeous sweaty body. "You know you want her to."

I swallowed nervously, and nodded.

"But you gotta keep licking me. As she said, that lipstick wont test itself."

I smiled, "Ok."

"And we don't want to ruin your gown."

"No." Was it a lucky gown? Was all this happening because I felt like looking like a beautiful princess tonight? I didn't know.

I slowly got to my feet, the pale blue satin of my gown rustling beautifully. Kayla got up off the sofa as well. I could smell her hot perfume on her glowing sexy body. I so wanted to have a body like hers. Maybe with time I would.

Claire stood to one side, a tube of lube in her hand. Slowly she poured it along the blue dildo that had so recently fucked Kayla to orgasm. And she wanted to do the same with me.

Kayla undid the buttons at the back of my gown and then I felt thrills run through me as it slid down my arms, my matching blue corset, panties and stockings, to land in a frothy heap on the floor. I looked down at it, not wanting to see the two gorgeous girls I loved more than anything else in the world looking at me like I was still a man.

A finger found my chin and moved my head to one side. Kayla's soft lips found mine. Then she whispered, "You're a beautiful girl."

Emotion filled me up and I couldn't say anything.

"Who's gonna be fucked like a hot whore," she added, with a wicked smile.

Carefully I stepped my silver stilettos out of the gown, making sure to catch sight of my smooth feminine body encased in gorgeous satin lingerie in a mirror.

Kayla took my right hand and led me to the sofa. She climbed on it and sat on the top, her legs wide, her hairless cunt inviting me to lick her sensitive lips.

I got onto my knees in front of her, my head between her legs.

I heard Claire move behind me, then my blue satin panties were pulled to one side and soft fingers began to spread coolness around my freshly shaved sissycunt.

"Still ok with this?" she asked me from behind.

I nodded, "Yes. And… thank you."

"Tits like yours, can't mistake you for anything other than a girl now."

Before I could say anything Kayla grabbed my hair and pulled my face forwards, mashing it into her soft wet pussy.

Behind me the fingers slowly entered me as I licked and slurped Kayla's pussy juice.

There was a slight pause.

Then I gasped as Claire made me one of the girls.

***

Motel Sissy - 2

I could tell my co-workers were getting unhappy with me by the way they whispered behind my back and the looks they gave me. Not to mention the poor guy that shared an apartment with me. I was snappy and irritable and seven shades of bitchy. I knew what my problem was but couldn't ever, *ever* tell them. I was pretty sure men couldn't get PMT, but I, for one, could get PST – Pre-Sissy Tension. The only way to alleviate it, and get close to being back in my co-workers good books, was by being Tiffany and getting fucked like the sissy slut she was.

So it was that I nearly screamed aloud (and would've scared the life out of Sally sitting next at the desk next to me) when I saw that the office I'd gone to last time needed some help. I didn't give a shit what the help was, hell, I didn't know if I could even help. The important part was to stay at the same motel where Tiffany discovered she had needs, and wants, and could be herself.

I put my name forward and got an almost instantaneous confirmation email in return. Then I made the motel booking. My hands trembled as I tapped my details in and hoped they had a room available. If they didn't I suppose I could be Tiffany at some other place. But I got another green light. This was looking to be my day. The only other hurdle would be if the same receptionist was still there. If she was would she remember me? Or the humiliating things she made Tiffany do? I had to take the chance, for my sanity, and that of my co-workers and roommate.

But what should I pack? My French maid uniform, it went without saying, but what else? The new see-through frilly white babydoll nightie with matching panties I'd got off the internet? Oh, that would be so good to wear, so soft against my smooth skin. I was so far into PST I got a hard-on just thinking about what to take! Although I was pretty sure I hid it, and the pre-cum my cock smeared on the inside of the pretty panties I wore, from my co-workers.

Back at my shared apartment Tiffany's case was almost bursting at the seams with gorgeous feminine lingerie and slutty outfits, while my other case contained the boring male stuff I had to wear.

~*~

Arriving at the motel some male I'd never seen before checked me in. I tried to look around for the lady that made me do such humiliating sissy things last time but I couldn't see her. I also felt it best not to ask about her as I had no idea what her name was, and describing her as someone's whose hot pussy I'd licked previously was a non-starter.

Luckily at the office Tiffany took a back seat and I managed to help without biting anyone's head off, and also avoided going out for a drink with anyone. I'd probably got a reputation by now and they were wondering why I'd volunteered to help without participating in any after work socialising. That was not what I was interested in.

When I'd finished and got back to the motel I got out of the hire car, hopefully remembering to lock it behind me, and walked into the motel. My heart was thumping like it was trying to escape from my chest. I possibly said something to whoever was at reception but if asked wouldn't be able to remember what it was or who was there. My hard erection pulled me along the corridor to my room. Would she be inside? Or would she wait until I'd got dressed in my frilly sissy finery?

I opened the door. The lights were off. I closed the door behind me and leant back against it. No strange perfume scented the air. The room had that empty feeling. I turned the lights on and saw everything was as I'd left it. Walking round the corner I saw clothes lying on the bed, but they weren't those I'd brought in Tiffany's case. Not the short pleated plaid skirt, the cropped white blouse, or white lace-trimmed bra, garter and panty set. Nor even the wig with side pigtails. And especially not the pink-jewelled butt-plug. I let a breath out I hadn't realised I'd been holding. She was still here. And she wanted to play with Tiffany.

Looking closer I saw she'd also been in Tiffany's case and taken out a new box of white lace-top hold-up stockings, a tube of lube for the butt-plug, and my fuck-me shiny red stilettos.

Underneath the butt-plug I found a note-

The Headmistress expects Tiffany in Room seven for her detention.

So, I wasn't going to be a sexy French maid. Instead I'd been a naughty college girl. And was going to be punished.

~*~

I carefully opened the door. Was anyone around to see slutty college girl Tiffany?

No.

A little voice in me asked what the fuck I was doing, dressed like this, going to see someone I didn't really know (apart from the aforementioned clit-licking), to do god-knows what? But Tiffany had been quiet for too long and wouldn't be denied her humiliating sissy desires. The proof of that was her erection pushing against the white cotton lace-trimmed panties and forcing them up between her smooth ass cheeks and sliding against the end of the butt-plug.

My room was 35, but where was room seven? Opposite me was 36. Further along to the left was 38. Therefore seven would be to my right. But how far? How far would Tiffany have to go with the chance of being seen?

Not hearing any voice or sounds of movement I closed the door behind me. The butt-plug moving in my ass would only let me take small scurrying steps along the hallway in my red stilettos.

A cool breeze found my uncovered torso, my freshly shaved stockinged legs, and flowed up my barely-there plaid skirt. My pigtails bounced off my shoulders and large breasts barely contained by my cropped white blouse.

Desperately I counted the door numbers, my ears open for any sound of people coming along the hallway or out of their rooms. I passed room 20 and stopped before turning a corner. I peered round, my long dark eyelashes flapping.

Still no-one.

Anyone behind me eyeing the jewelled butt-plug and ass cheeks of a big-breasted slutty college girl?

No.

I sped past the doors until I came to room seven. Dare I knock? What would she make me, or rather Tiffany, do? I stood undecided in the hallway. Then Tiffany made the decision for me and knocked.

"Hello? Who is it?" a female voice said from inside.

Was I at the right door? Had I read the card correctly? I didn't have it on me. I suppose I could've tucked it into my bra like I did my room's key-card. I glanced round the hallway, no other door had 7 on it.

I made sure to soften my voice before saying, "It's me, um, Tiffany, Miss?"

"What are you here for, Tiffany?"

"Detention, Miss?"

"Why?"

"Er, I've been naughty, Miss?"

The door opened. It was the same lady that made me do such humiliating things last time I stayed here. She had her hair up in a tight bun and wore a dark red satin pussy-bow blouse, a knee-length black leather skirt, nylons and shiny red heels that matched her blouse. She looked gorgeous.

"Tiffany?"

"Yes, Miss."

"You look very pretty."

I glowed inside.

"Thank you, Miss. So do you."

She smiled at the compliment, then said, "Are you properly dressed for detention?"

What did she mean by that? And could she let me in so I'd not potentially be seen by anyone?

"Um, yes, Miss?"

"Turn around and bend over, Tiffany."

Oh, the jewelled butt-plug.

I quickly turned around and bent over, then reached round and lifted the hem on my short plaid skirt with one hand and used my other to pull my panties down to show her the jewel end of the butt plug that was moving so deliciously inside of me.

I heard people start talking from along the corridor and quickly stood up, letting go of my skirt and panties, and turned around.

She still stood there, with a thin smile on her face and a glint in her eye. I knew she could hear them as well. But why wasn't she letting me enter?

"Please, Miss!" I frantically whispered, trying to pull my short skirt lower so that I didn't look so much like a college girl slut.

The voices came closer and closer. It sounded like a man and woman. I turned to look. How close were they?

Suddenly my arm was grabbed and she yanked me into the room and quickly closed the door.

~*~

I breathed a sigh of relief, hearing the voices pass by the closed door. I was safe from being seen. But now I wondered what she was going to do with me.

"Into my office, Tiffany."

"Yes, Mistress," I said in my feminine Tiffany voice.

As well as the room's bed a wooden school desk met my eyes as I walked round the corner.

"Stand there," she ordered, indicating the centre of the room.

"Yes, Miss."

I shuffled over to it and stood still, my hands clasped nervously in front of me, my butt plug making my erection and balls go nuts. I definitely felt like a naughty college girl called to the headmistress's office.

Slowly she walked around me, flicking my ponytails, feeling my cotton blouse, straightening my short plaid skirt. Then she sat down at the desk and put some glasses on.

The desk had the standard lamp, but also a mobile phone and a brown folder. She pressed a button on the phone and then pulled the folder towards her and opened it.

"This is your report, Tiffany."

"Miss."

She fixed me with a glare. "It doesn't make good reading, Tiffany."

"No, Miss. Er, sorry, Miss."

I looked shamefacedly down at my shiny red stilettos.

"Have you always been a slut, Tiffany?" she said sternly.

I looked up in surprise, "Miss?"

She took her glasses off and used them to point at a part of the report. "It says here that you keep bending over in front of the male staff to show off your breasts and backside."

What could I say? "Sorry, Miss?"

"Sorry doesn't cut it, Tiffany."

"No, Miss."

"And this part here where it says you add inappropriate comments to your essays."

"Miss?"

She gave me another stern look, then put her glasses back on and turned back to Tiffany's report. "In your essay concerning Shakespeare you stated you wanted to suck huge cocks before being fucked like a cheap street whore over a desk."

Tiffany wrote that? She was such a slut! "Miss. Sorry, Miss."

"Deliberate sexual enticement of the male staff is prohibited, Tiffany."

"It is?"

"Yes."

"Oh."

"And I'm disgusted to say that there's also sexual enticement to the female staff."

This was unexpected. "Miss?"

"Apparently you wish to rub your clit against a certain female teacher's nylon-clad legs."

I was so surprised I couldn't say anything.

"Nothing to say about that, Tiffany?"

I gaped at her like a fish.

She turned back to me and crossed her legs, her leather skirt squeaking slightly and her nylons shushing as they slid over each other.

"Well, Tiffany?"

"M… Miss?" I whispered.

"I think you need a little pleasure before your detention begins in earnest." She gave me a look over the top of her glasses. "Before I change my mind, Tiffany."

"Miss."

I shuffled over until my stocking-clad legs were either side of her crossed one and our nylons were gently touching then lifted the hem of my short plaid skirt. My hard erection pushed against the front of my lace-edged white cotton panties. I could feel the coolness of wet-precum at the tip.

Slowly, not expecting what her reaction would be, I slid the head of my erection side to side over her nylon-clad knee. Thrills ran through my erection and butt-plug as it moved deep within me, and into my balls.

"Do you like my blouse, Tiffany?"

"Yes, Miss, it's so pretty."

"Do you like wearing pretty, feminine blouses, Tiffany?"

"Yes, Miss. Wearing something beautiful makes me feel so happy, Miss."

"And my leather skirt?"

"Definitely, Miss. I love wearing skirts."

"Would you like to wear skirts and pretty tops and blouses every day?"

"It would be a dream come true, Miss."

I moved so that my heavy balls were rubbing against her knee and just catching the hem of her leather skirt. It felt so good. My erection was so hard. I closed my eyes savouring the feel of my butt-plug moving and my balls and the different fabrics rubbing against each other.

"Are you going to orgasm, Tiffany?"

Startled, I jerked back. "No, Miss!"

"Hmm. It looked like you were. And that is precisely why you've been given detention, Tiffany."

"Yes, Miss."

"But I feel that mere detention won't make any difference to your actions, Tiffany."

"No, Miss?"

"No. I feel that a taste of the cane on your backside will make the message loud and clear."

She was going to cane me! I'd never been caned before! Would it hurt? Well, I guess it would. But how much?

She stood up and took out a thin round handled cane that had been hidden behind the desk. She used it to indicate the wooden desk in the centre of the room. "Turn around and bend over the desk, Tiffany."

Fear grew in me at being caned, "Miss! I won't do it again, Miss!"

But her stern voice brooked no nonsense. "Bend over, Tiffany."

I shuffled over to the desk and held onto the sides to bend over, feeling my butt-plug move deliciously within me, and the garter belt straps press into my ass cheeks. My erection slid against my precum as it squashed against the wood through the thin cotton panties.

I watched her legs as they slowly walked to my left side. Then I felt the hem of my short plaid skirt being lifted up and laid on top of my ass.

She was really going to do this!

"Legs apart, and hold on to the top of the desk, Tiffany."

I moved as ordered and felt the panty gusset ride up further between my ass cheeks and press against the butt-plug jewel.

"Are you wearing a thong, Tiffany?"

"No, Miss. They're panties, Miss!"

"Only whores wear thongs, Tiffany. It appears your report is incomplete."

"Miss! Please, Miss!"

"What did you write about hard cocks, Tiffany?"

What was she after? "Sorry, Miss?"

Swish!

Pain exploded in my ass, forcing my hard erection painfully against the wooden desk. My hands gripped the top of the desk as if they were going to rip it off.

I cried out, not caring if anyone heard me.

It felt like my ass cheeks were on fire.

Then it came to me, "Miss! I wanted to suck them and get fucked like a street whore over a desk, Miss!"

"Do you like sucking a man's erection until they cum in your mouth, Tiffany?"

"Yes, Miss!"

Swish!

I cried out feeling my ass cheeks burn even hotter.

"Why?"

"It makes me feel so feminine to know I've made a man orgasm, Miss!"

Swish!

The pain was unbearable!

"Why are you wearing such slutty clothes?"

"To make men notice me and want to fuck me, Miss!"

Before she could cane me again a tone sounded from behind me. What was it?

"Had enough, Tiffany?"

"Yes, Miss!"

"Stay there, Tiffany."

I sighed with relief. "Yes, Miss."

She walked back to the desk and picked her phone up. After tapping a few keys she put it back down.

What was she going to do now? I didn't think my burning ass cheeks could take much more caning.

She walked past me to the bed where I'd not noticed a black leather bag sitting on it. What was in store for Tiffany now?

"I got these for just this occasion, Tiffany."

"Miss?"

She pulled out something black and shiny and unwrapped them to show they were a pair of black satin panties, but they had something pale on them.

"After having read your report I persuaded one of the male staff to ejaculate onto a pair of my used panties. And as your report tells me how much of a slut you are I'm sure you'll be able to tell me how fresh this sperm is."

She wanted me to sniff another man's semen?

Walking in front of me she dangled the cum-spattered panties in front of my face. The smell of jizz was unmistakeable.

"Taste it, Tiffany. Taste a man's sperm and tell me how fresh it is."

Oh.

"Or do you need a little persuasion? Shall I start caning you again?"

I quickly leant forwards and licked at the pale cum. Salt hit my tongue and filled my mouth. I had another man's sperm in my mouth! Shame burned through me.

"That's a good slut. Lick them clean, Tiffany."

I didn't want to be caned again so my tongue greedily lapped up the thick salty cum that some unknown man had jizzed onto the black satin panties. I felt it smear over my glossy red lips and swallowed it, feeling it slide down my throat and increase the hot burning shame at what I was doing.

"Is it all gone, Tiffany? Have you licked my used panties clean?"

"Yes, Miss."

"Good girl. How fresh was it?"

"Very, Miss."

"I know a slut like yourself would've much rather sucked a hard cock to get a hot load of sperm, wouldn't you?"

"Yes, Miss."

"You still have sperm smeared on your lips, Tiffany. Be a good girl and lick it off."

"Sorry, Miss."

I licked my glossy red lips of the smeared cum and swallowed the salty mixture down.

"Do you know what I'm going to do with these now, Tiffany?"

"No, Miss."

She stood closer to me and tied the panties around my head, covering my eyes, blindfolding me. Why did she do that?

"Can you see, Tiffany?"

I could feel the damp patch where I'd licked the semen off them, and could smell a mix of her pussy scent and the cum on them.

"No, Miss."

"Good."

I jumped at hearing a knock at the door. OMG! Someone else was coming in! To see me bending over a desk, dressed like a college girl slut! But they would also see my balls and erection underneath my panties! They'll know I'm a sissy slut!

"I wonder who that is, Tiffany. Stay there."

"Miss!" I whispered, horrified.

I heard her walk away from me and then open the door. Voices whispered but I couldn't make out what was said.

The door closed and I heard the steps of two people walk round the corner to see me bent over a desk, my freshly caned ass cheeks in plain view.

"As you can see headmaster, Tiffany is taking part in her detention. From her report I notice that you were the male colleagues she was teasing with her ass and breasts. Now she's being punished I think it only fair you take her up on her offer."

I heard a pair of feet walking around and stop in front of me. Then the unmistakeable sound of a zip undoing.

I was going to suck another man's cock!

"As she's such a whore I think you should start by cock slapping her face. I know she'll love the feel of a hard erection showing her where she stands. Or, in this case, bent over."

I heard the sound of fabric being moved and then a slight musky scent. Was his erection pointing towards my face?

A hand lifted my chin up and then *Slap*!

Something large and hard suddenly hit my right cheek.

"Just like that, headmaster. Now the other side."

Slap!

OMG! Some unknown man was cock slapping me!

"Now rub it over her mouth."

Something hot and hard rubbed itself over my glossy lips, smearing the remains of the cum I'd licked off the panties.

"Open your mouth, Tiffany."

I could guess what would happen next, and I didn't want it to happen. But I knew she had no problem with caning me.

"Put your balls in her mouth, headmaster. Let her feel how heavy with sperm she's made them."

Something large and warm was pushed into my mouth. I had to move my tongue out of the way or it would've gag me. I felt two balls jiggling around in their sac, and felt a humiliating jerk in my panties. Warmth burned my cheeks as I knew I was dripping precum.

"Suck them, Tiffany," she whispered close to my head. "Suck his balls. You're such a slut you want to drain them of lovely hot cum.

Humiliating tears stung my blindfolded eyes as I did as told, feeling forbidden excitement run through my own balls and erection.

A deep groan came from above my head.

"Keep sucking his balls, Tiffany."

I did as told and heard her walk behind me to the desk. What was going on now?

I heard some taps on the phone and then she said, "Your detention is proving very popular, Tiffany."

What did she mean by that?

"I'll just take some photos to pass around the staff to show that you're taking your punishment like a good girl."

What? No!

I heard the unmistakeable *click!* sound of a mobile phone camera being used.

What pictures was she taking? I didn't want people seeing me dressed as a college girl slut bend over a desk with a butt-plug in my caned red ass and sucking another man's balls!

I tried to push them out with my tongue but my head was held tightly and I couldn't get rid of them!

"Now, now, Tiffany. Do you want me to cane you again?"

No, I didn't.

"Put your cock in her mouth, headmaster."

He pulled his balls out of my mouth and quickly stuck something long, wide, and hard in their place.

"Hold steady, that'll make a lovely picture for the staffroom wall."

No!

But the phone clicked. What was she going to do with them?

"Fuck her mouth, headmaster. Make her feel like the slut she is."

My head was held tightly as he started forcing his cock deeper and deeper into my mouth.

"If you're happy fucking her mouth, headmaster, I'll prepare her cunt for the second part of her detention. We must make sure she is suitably punished for her transgressions."

I felt my white cotton panties being pulled out from between my ass cheeks and then jerked as she started toying with the jewelled butt-plug in my ass. I could only moan as she stretched my ass wider with the plug because I had a hard erection stuffing my mouth and pushing to go down my throat.

My legs nearly failed me and I think I squealed as she pulled the plug almost all of the way out but then pushed it back in.

The precum soaking my white cotton panties had now reached my balls, and I felt its coolness smear against them. Why was I enjoying this humiliating experience so much?

"Play with her soft lips, headmaster."

The cock was pulled almost all of the way out leaving just the mushroom head in my mouth. Slowly just the head was pushed in and out so that my soft lips rubbed against the edge. More groans of pleasure came from above me.

Then she started playing with my butt-plug in earnest, pulling it almost all of the way out, pushing it back in, quickly, slowly, until my own cock and balls felt like they were going to explode.

"She's ready, headmaster."

The butt-plug was completely removed and I felt the cool addition of more lubricant. Then the cock was pulled from my mouth. But before my ass could close up the headmaster moved round and pushed it into my ass. My mind flashed to images of sexy whores being fucked from behind up against walls as I felt his jeans rubbing against the insides of my stockinged legs. His balls bounced against mine still hiding in my lace-trimmed white cotton panties.

Oh god. A man was using me. Fucking me.

Slowly the thrusts in and out began to speed up. Unbelievable sensations fired through my body.

"Squeeze Tiffany's clit, headmaster, she's meant to be punished during detention."

I gasped with surprise as a hand gripped my cock through my wet panties, found my cockhead, and began squeezing it, pushing the blood back out of it!

They weren't going to allow me to cum?

The sensations flowing from my fucked ass seemed to intensify. Did squeezing my erection away make the feeling of a hard erection fucking my ass feel so good?

Suddenly a soft hand cupped my chin and something warm and damp and musky was forced against my face.

"Lick me, Tiffany," she moaned from above my head.

My tongue flicked out and lapped at her wet pussy, tasting her juice. She gasped with pleasure and then began grinding her hot cunt against my face, trying to get my tongue deeper, smearing her scent over me.

Gasps came from behind me as my fucking sped up. The hand had squeezed my erection now to almost nothing, and it was now gripping my balls through the lace-edged cotton panties as well. My whole maleness was being controlled by, and held within, a man's hand. I wasn't a man I was a sissy girl, being fucked by a man.

And I loved it.

I moaned like a desperate whore into the soft wet pussy my head was being forced against.

"Are you nearly cumming, headmaster?" she gasped. "Are you going to cum in Tiffany's cunt?"

Oh please, yes! Please cum in Tiffany's cunt!

I gripped hold of the desk and pushed back against the hard cock, wanting it deeper and deeper into Tiffany's wet cunt. Wanting more pleasure from it. Wanting to be fucked like a girl. Wanting to be fucked by a man.

That was the tipping point as the cock was pushed as deep into me as it could go and I felt his leg muscles suddenly tense against mine, then a gasp sounded from behind me and I felt something hot and liquid fire deep into my ass.

A man had just shot his load into my cunt!

An orgasm hit me and I gasped into her wet pussy, but I couldn't shoot my own load as two fingers of the tightly gripping hand were pinching my limp dick closed, preventing me from ejaculating. My balls desperately jerked as the orgasm washed over me but nothing could come out!

But how was I orgasming?

His legs jerked again and again and I felt more hot cum in my cunt. I squealed like a slut riding my orgasm, my heart hammering.

What was happening? I'd never felt anything like this before!

Eventually his ejaculations into my cunt slowed down and I felt the loads of hot semen start to flow towards the exit.

"Put the plug back in," she gasped from above me. "Let her walk around with your sperm in her cunt like the slut she is."

The hand released my limp clit and balls and I felt it wipe my precum off on my short plaid skirt. The still hard erection was pulled out of my ass and then the smooth metal of the butt-plug replaced it, trapping his cum in my cunt.

My panties sprang back into position, gently holding the plug in place.

She moved back and I felt the cooler air against my pussy-juice smeared face.

The sound of a zip being pulled up came from behind me, and then footsteps around the corner and the door opening and closing.

It was then I felt something strange happen in my dick. Now it was released the pent-up cum that had been held back in my balls was now starting flow.

"I'm cumming?" I whispered.

I heard her walk to the bed and rummage around in her bag for something, then walk back to me. Something tapped my right hand. "You might need a panty-liner, Tiffany."

"Thank you."

"Keep the slutty clothes and plug for next time, Tiffany."

"Yes, Miss."

Then the sound of her steps followed those of the headmaster and the door closed behind her.

I could still feel his hand gripping my dick and balls as my cum flowed out of my limp dick and soak the front of my panties, even more so than my precum previously did.

Thoughts swirled around in my head – the feel of his hand gripping my manhood, my orgasm being controlled by another man, the feeling of his cock in my mouth and being thrust in and out of my ass, being used as a sissy cumslut, the orgasm I'd had when he fucked me.

It was then I knew one thing.

Tiffany was his bitch.

***

Channel Sissy

Discovered

I had no idea what my new neighbour did for a living. I mean I worked at a dreary job in the city, but her? I'd never known her to match my nine-to-five, but she still managed to afford an apartment in the same block as me. How'd that happen? Rich parents? An amazing alimony? Not a clue.

All I knew was that she was hot. Her luscious dark hair seemed to have a natural wave to it, her sexy curves were mind-numbing, her face could've graced any perfume ad. And my dick thanked whatever gods were hanging around each time I saw her.

So, if asked why I wore her thong I couldn't really give an answer. It was hers. It smelt of the softener she used. Just having something of hers seemed to fill an unknown hole I had in my soul. I could've just stuck it in a pocket and took it our every so often to sniff and remind myself of her. But wear it? I guess there was something sexual about it. I mean I'd rubbed it against my dick and enjoyed its smooth softness on the way to an orgasm. Maybe that was the only way I'd get close to her? It seemed that the next (il)logical step was to wear it, so my masculine cock could feel her soft smooth femininity all the time.

I suppose that was why I got an erection when sliding her pink satin thong up my legs.

I also liked wearing her thong because both my balls didn't fit inside so they sort of hung out either side of the string and jiggled around when I walked.

Previously we'd just exchanged a polite 'Morning' when we saw each other in the hallway. But now I wore her thong - something intimate of hers. And here I was looking for more of her clothes to wear.

I bent down to look into the front-loading washing machine, feeling my jeans move down exposing the back of her thong. Had she left anything in the apartment block's basement laundry room this Sunday morning? I spun the empty drum.

No.

Oh well. At least I'd got the thong. I'd timed my visit to the laundry just a few minutes after she'd finished this week's load to make sure no-one else had a chance of finding something of hers. But it looked to be a bust.

"So that's where they are!" cried an angry voice from behind me.

I sprang back up to my feet and turned round. She stood in front of me, a blaze of fury on her face, still holding the basket of dry washing she'd left with barely a few minutes ago. She was only slightly shorter than me but at that moment it felt like she towered over me.

"What the fuck are you wearing my clothes for?"

"I… I…" I stammered, my shameful mind blank in the face of her beautiful scary anger.

Her shoulder-length dark hair was in a rough ponytail and she still wore the black miniskirt with the zip at the back and those dark tights and trainers I'd seen her in that morning. The black skinny sweater she wore totally failed to hide her gorgeous breasts.

"What kind of sick fuck are you?"

I felt a burning in my cheeks. I was blushing? "I… I'm sorry. I could give them back–?"

She interrupted, "Why the fuck would I want them back after you've worn them?"

"Um…" Her beautiful brown eyes glared into mine and I felt something move in her pink satin thong I wore. No, even without knowing what I'd used them for previously, she'd definitely not want them back now.

I cleared my throat, "I'm sorry. I could get you some more? I've got some money on me I could pay you for them?"

"You want to buy my underwear?" her eyes looked down at what was happening in my jeans. "Oh, god. You're getting an erection in them?"

My cheeks felt so hot now that I was sure if someone cracked an egg onto them it'd burn to a crisp.

"You fucking disgust me. Getting off wearing… Jesus! Wait, what's that word?"

What?

"Sissy? You're a sissy. You get off wearing female clothes!"

Sissy? What the fuck was she going on about? "No. I'm not a sissy." I wasn't sure what a sissy was but I knew I definitely wasn't one!

She looked at me, and then down at the bulge in my jeans.

"Sure looks like it from here. So? Are you?"

"Fuck off, no."

She poked me in the chest with her right forefinger. "Don't fucking lie to me. Are you one of those sick fucks that gets off wearing lingerie and dresses?"

"No!"

Her hand flashed forwards and grabbed my erection through my jeans. I cried out in surprise. "Ow! Get off me!"

"Fucking say it!"

"No!"

"Say it! Say you're a sissy!"

I tried to bat her hand away from my cock but she moved the washing basket in the way.

"All right! I'm a sissy. Fucking happy now?"

"Good. Take them down."

"What?"

I cried out again as she viciously jerked my erection.

"Ow!"

"Take these down, show me my thong."

"What? Ow!"

She let me go after one last jerk and I hurriedly undid my belt and jeans button then unzipped. My sore erection bulged against the pink satin thong.

"Hold still."

"What?"

Before I knew what was happening she'd whipped her phone out from a back pocket and snapped a picture of me. Why the hell would she do that?

Then she turned round and left, with her basket of washing held against her hip with her left hand and tapping away on her mobile with her right.

It felt like a storm had just passed. I took some deep breaths trying to process what had just happened. Then I realised the pink satin thong I wore was still in plain view of anyone entering the room. Quickly I zipped back up and got myself together then headed back up to my apartment.

Over the next few days I tried not to think about what had happened, immersing myself into whatever TV shows people were talking about. I even made a solemn vow not to visit the laundry after she'd used it. Somehow I even got my head round the shit that was going on at work.

And then the note appeared.

The note

I'd come home from work and opened my door to find a folded piece of paper lying on the floor that had been slipped under it.

Not suspecting anything, just puzzled as to what it was about, I picked it up and opened it. A photo fell out and landed on the floor. I looked down at myself with a shocked expression on my face with pink satin showing through my jeans zipper.

Oh God.

I read the note. It was short and devastating, like a sucker punch to the gut.

See you at 8pm. Wear them. Or else.

I dropped my backpack and slumped down to the cold floor, my back literally against a wall.

What could I do? I'd been brought up to apologize for doing things wrong. I'd go see her and apologize and maybe she wouldn't make this go any further. I could see if I could get her some sort of prepaid giftcard to make up for taking her thong? Something from an expensive store. She'd probably like something like that. Yes. That's what I'd do. I'd 'Man up' as the saying went. Maybe if I played my cards right this could be start of something nice? Who knew?

My decision made I picked myself and the photo up off the floor. As I'd been late at work I had a quick drink of juice, then changed from my suit and tie and shoes into jeans a sweatshirt and trainers, and grabbed the thong that had caused the problem in the first place in my jeans pocket. I wasn't going to wear them ever again. I'd been taught a lesson. My dick reminded me how painful the lesson had been.

I knocked on her door at precisely 8pm. The sharp sound loud in the empty hallway.

Silence.

Was she in? Should I try again? Maybe she was in the bathroom and didn't hear? Should I leave and try again later? Maybe leave a note? What to do? What to do?

I'd try again. Maybe it was the bathroom thing. I raised my hand again, and the door opened.

She looked beautiful in a knee-length ruffled sleeveless red dress with plunging neckline, her dark hair loose, the merest hint of make up. The subtle scent she wore ensnared me. Did she wear this for me?

Stunned, my dick bursting into life, I stammered, "H… hi."

Without a word, or a smile, she opened the door further, inviting me in.

"Thank you," I said. Be polite, you've wronged her. This is the time to make things right.

I walked in and looked around the sitting room. It looked like she went in for the minimalist theme, with just a few pictures on the walls, small statues and vases on small tables–

Closing the door behind her she interrupted my thoughts with,

"You wearing them?"

I stopped and turned to her. "Um, about that? I'm really–"

Her beautiful eyes went hard. "Sissy's not wearing his pink satin thong?"

My hand went to the pocket where I'd put them. "No, I–"

"You're here so you did get the note."

"Yes?"

"You read the 'or else' part?"

"Well, yes. I just thought–"

She walked past me in a whirl of beautiful scent, her dress swishing around her flawless legs and stopped at a table with a laptop open on it. She tapped a key and a TV screen on the wall sprang to life. It showed the picture of me she'd taken and my name and phone number. How'd she get my name and phone number?

"What?" I turned to her.

She glared at me. "This is the 'or else' part. Put them on or this goes online and your life, as the Chinese say, gets interesting."

I was speechless and could only manage a "But?"

Her right forefinger swirled above the enter key on her laptop.

I tried again, "You'd–?"

She raised a perfect eyebrow and slowly lowered her finger to the enter key.

"Wait!"

I kicked my trainers off and took the pink thong out of my pocket. Then turned round and took my jeans off and then my boxers. Leaving them piled on the floor I tried to work out which bit went where on the thong. Eventually I think I worked it out and stepped into them, then slid them up my legs. The smooth pink satin barely held my balls and semi-erect cock. The string back naturally found its way between my cheeks.

"Turn round."

I sighed, hoping this would be the end of it.

She sat at the table, one leg over the other and had turned the laptop so its top faced me. The TV screen now showed me wearing the thong and my sweater. She'd linked the laptop's video to the TV?

"You like wearing pink satin thongs?"

I sighed. This again. "No."

"Your erection says otherwise. Or is it you think I'm hot?"

"Are you saving this?" I indicated the TV screen, and avoiding the question.

"Uh huh. Me and the girls will have a laugh at this next time we get together."

It didn't look like my plan would bear fruit. My heart fell. "What will it take to end this?"

She gave me a puzzled look. "But your dick says you enjoy wearing female clothes?"

"This is the first time and I'm never going to do it again."

She corrected me, "Second, hon. Once was enough to show me you're a sissy."

"Second. And last. And I'm not."

"What if I said I had a matching pink satin bra you could wear?"

My erection began to strain against the pink satin thong.

She nodded to herself at the sight, "Uh huh. Or what about a frilly pink babydoll?"

"No. I won't wear it– them," I hastily added, then remembered to be polite and added, "Thank you."

"Take your top off."

"What?"

"You heard me." Her finger swirled over the enter key again.

I sighed and took my top off, feeling the cooler air swirl round my torso.

"Good, Sissy."

"I'm not a sissy."

She ignored my protest and reached down beside her into a plain black bag by her feet.

"Look how pretty this is." She brought out a see-through frilly pink babydoll nightie. "It matches the thong, don't you think?"

My dick did think so and I felt a coolness at its tip pressing against the pink satin covering it.

"Aw, so sweet," she said, seeing the darker patch of my precum on the shiny pink material.

Holding the babydoll up before her she got up and walked over to me, like a lioness stalking its prey.

"Would it help if I said I'd worn this?"

"No." But my dick said otherwise.

"So you do think I'm hot."

My mind hastily tried to change gear, and failed. "No, but yes, I do. But I'm not wearing it." Did that even come out right?

She was so close now that it gently brushed against my bare chest.

"Feel how soft and gentle it is," she whispered. "How it excites your nipples, and sends thrills to your hard, so so hard, erection."

My cock was now so hard that the thong was now pulled tightly between my cheeks.

"Imagine wearing something so soft and pretty and feminine," she continued whispering. I felt her breasts press it harder against me. "Are your nipples hard? Mine are."

Her feminine fragrance wrapped itself around me. And pulled tight.

"No."

"Your erection says otherwise. Give in to your urges."

It was like listening to the siren's song of ancient Greek myth. I had to be strong.

She lifted it up and slid it over my head. Then took gentle hold of my right wrist and slid it through the armhole. Then repeated it with my left wrist.

"There. Doesn't that feel so nice?" her voice was so soft and quiet.

It did. It felt like I wore a cloud, its softness sent beautiful feelings around my body.

She moved around to my right and I wondered what she was doing. But soon found out with a surprised jerk when she took hold of my erection through the satin thong and gently pumped it up and down.

I was in a haze of swirling pleasure. A beautiful woman was masturbating me. Excitement built up in my balls and cock. The thong's string was wedged tightly between my cheeks.

Suddenly the feelings intensified and I gasped out feeling my cock explode in an orgasm!

Oh my God! What just happened?

I felt my hot semen slide against my cock head as it hit the pink satin barrier. I looked down past the frilly pink satin babydoll to see my cum seeping through the pink satin.

I looked up at the TV screen seeing a man wearing a filly babydoll nightie with cum dripping from his pink satin thong.

What had she done?

I looked at her and saw her smile. But it wasn't a nice smile.

Fear filled me and I quickly bent down and grabbed my clothes and rushed to the door, yanking it open and fleeing to my apartment, slamming the door shut behind me.

My heart hammering, I dropped my trainers and clothes on the floor and rushed into the bathroom. I turned the shower on and got in it not caring what temperature it was. Then realised I still wore the babydoll and thong. I ripped them off me and flung them onto the floor. I grabbed the shower gel and scrubbed the shameful cum off my genitals.

What had she done?

Why had she done it?

I stood, thoughts whirling in my head, under the shower that was now getting to the normal temperature I used. It was only then that I realised I'd had a cold shower to begin with.

What was going on with the video on the TV?

Was she going to blackmail me? Would I have to leave the apartment? The city? My job?

Was there a way out of this?

I didn't know. But I knew one thing. The shameful clothes on the bathroom floor were going in the trash. I never wanted to see them ever again.

Like some unthinking automaton I existed through the next few days. I probably ate, slept, went to work, lived some sort of life. But it didn't register with my mind.

And then the email appeared.

The email

I'd been collating information from the company's other offices and mindlessly opened the email attachment. I thought it was a bit strange that a video program started up but figured whoever sent the email wanted to say something about the information they'd sent.

I think I closed it before anyone else saw me wearing the see-through frilly pink babydoll. Definitely before I orgasmed. Yes, definitely.

After a few deep breaths to calm my racing heart I looked at the sender's address. Nothing I recognised, and nothing at all to do with the company I worked for.

My inbox showed I had another email from the same address. But it didn't show it had any attachments. I opened it up. The message was short-

See you at 8pm. Wear the thong and babydoll. Or else.

"Wear what?" came a voice from beside me.

"What?!" I almost screamed, jumping up from my chair. It was Cassidy from the desk beside mine. How much had she seen?

"Jesus, sorry! Just wondered what they wanted you to wear."

I had to think fast or she'd know something was wrong. "I... I..." Cassidy wore glasses. "Eyes... Contacts, glasses.

No, contacts. It's from my mum, she says I've got to wear contacts. Or it's glasses."

She gave me a look like I'd just taken a step onto the first rung of her weirdo-meter ladder. "Uh huh. You ok? I mean this report stuff can get to you?"

I smiled apologetically, my heart rate slowing down from the buzz-saw it had been, "Sorry. Sorry, should be ok soon."

"Ok." She went back to her own desk. "Don't forget to wear them, ok? Sight's important."

"Right."

Thankfully it wasn't long before I could finish for the day. But what could I do? My neighbour had a video of me orgasming while wearing lingerie. Which I'd then torn off my body in disgust and thrown away vowing to never wear it again. Could I take the risk she'd not send the email with the video attachment to everyone in the company? How'd she get hold of my work email address anyway?

But what would happen if I went to her apartment without the babydoll and pink satin thong? What would she do to me? Or make me do?

There was only one thing I could do – buy the same lingerie.

There was no time for me to order them online. I'd have to go to a shop and hope they had the same set. Were they a set? I didn't know. But would she accept me in a set that was a close match?

Oh crap, fuckingfucking crap! The stuff she was making me do!

Were there any shops that sold lingerie I could get to on the way home? Would I have time to get them? Not a clue. Oh, god I'd have to ask someone.

I cleared my throat and whispered, "Hey, Cassidy?"

She glanced at me wondering If I'd stepped up onto the next weirdo-meter rung. "Yeah?"

"Sorry about earlier. I've got stuff on my mind. Um, can I ask a shopping question?"

"Shopping?"

"Yeah. I want to get something special for someone. Um… a female someone. Are there any stores nearby?"

"Depends what you're looking for."

Ah.

I surreptitiously looked around me like I was in a bad spy movie. Then dry swallowed and croaked, "A frilly pink babydoll nightie and pink satin thong."

She sat back in her chair and looked at me. I could tell I'd just jumped several rungs.

"A–?" she began.

But I quickly interrupted, "Yeah. Um, I'd appreciate it if this could be kept, you know, quiet?"

"Uh huh."

My heart almost stopped when I saw her open her bottom desk draw and reach into her bag. Was she going to pepper-spray me? But she brought out her phone and started swiping it.

"Somewhere close by?" I added, hopefully.

"Uh huh. What size?"

Oh.

"Um, she's biggish. I guess… sort of… my size? Yeah, about my size. Big girl. Yeah?"

She glanced at me. I was within reach of the top now.

"Something like these?" She held the phone out to me. They didn't look to be the exact shade of pink but things always looked slightly different on screens.

"Yeah, that."

She took the phone back and swiped some more then held it out to me again. "I've reserved the largest size they have. Write this down."

She held the phone out to me again and I grabbed a pen and some paper and scribbled the address and order information down as if my life depended on it.

The lingerie department

I got to the store and rushed up the escalator to the lingerie department. It was like I'd entered a different world, one where the male of the species was a rarity and questions needed to be asked if they were even allowed to be there in the first place.

Thankfully I had some idea of where to go, and felt querying female eyes on me as I headed for a sign saying Order Collection.

A grey-haired elderly lady stood, all of her five foot nothing, behind the desk looking like she was clock-watching. I put my small backpack on the floor. "Hi, I'm here to pick an order up?"

She gave me the stink-eye and said, "Details, please."

I handed the scrap of paper over and she tapped the information into the computer. "A pink babydoll and matching thong?" Her face went blank like she was playing poker.

"Yes."

She turned to her side and called out, "Claudia?"

A younger lady with her glossy black hair held in a loose ponytail appeared from the dressing rooms, "Yes?"

"Could you pick an order up for this gentleman?"

"Certainly." She gave me a winning smile and I felt an answer in my boxers. She looked almost too sexy in the black pencil skirt and cream blouse as she came over and had a look at the screen. Her name badge jiggled on her chest pocket that covered her left breast.

"It's only just been added so there hasn't been time to hold it back," the older lady said.

Claudia shared a look with her colleague. Unfortunately the bulge in my trousers hadn't died down before she left the desk and headed into the racks of lingerie.

After a few moments she came back with a dark pink babydoll and a matching thong on hangers. Would that shade do? I didn't know.

"Um, is there anything less dark? More lighter pink?"

"Bright pink. In the same size?" The older lady asked, still poker-faced.

"Um, yeah?"

I felt Claudia's eyes on me and could tell she'd seen the bulge in my trousers. She shared another look with her colleague.

Would it be too obvious if I picked my backpack up and used it to hide my stiffy?

It didn't take Sherlock Holmes to know that they knew the items were for me. I couldn't deny it, or really say anything. I knew I wasn't a sissy. I was just being made to wear frilly babydolls and pink satin thongs by my neighbour. I didn't want to do it, but unfortunately I had to or my life would be much much worse. Just get over it, ok?

"We may have what the gentleman is looking for in the clearance section?" suggested Claudia.

"I'll keep these here in case there aren't any," Poker face replied.

"Ok."

Claudia walked away into the lingerie racks and I turned to see the older lady quickly glance up from my crotch.

I felt my cheeks warming. I had to say something, "It's not…" Then quickly thought better of saying anything even more incriminating than what I was already doing.

"Nearly the end of the day, Sir."

"Yes."

"Anything nice planned?"

No, just being humiliated by my neighbour into wearing frilly lingerie.

"No, um… just chilling out."

And by that I didn't mean I want to wear the lingerie I'm buying, ok?

Thankfully I was saved from more small talk by the arrival of the sexy Claudia and the correct shade of bright pink babydoll and satin thong.

It was at that moment my cock remembered cumming in the same lingerie yesterday, and desperately threw itself at the front of my boxers to try and get at the lingerie Claudia held. I felt my cheeks warming and quickly moved closer to the desk to try and hide my embarrassing bulge and hoped neither of them had seen it.

My throat went dry just as I was about to say that they were fine.

"Would sir like to purchase these items?" Poker face asked, taking them from Claudia. She was a bitch and I could tell she was enjoying my embarrassment.

I swallowed. "Yes, those will be fine, thank you."

Reaching below the desk, and possibly getting an eyeful of my erection, she pulled out a bag with the shop's name emblazoned on it. She carefully folded the babydoll and placed the thong on it, then slid them into the bag.

"They feel so soft and delicate, sir."

Yeah, yeah. Fuck right off.

I handed my credit card over and tapped the pin in all the while trying to hide my erection from their sight.

As soon as everything was done I took the bag, picked up my backpack and hurried away, using them to cover my crotch and the bulge in my trousers. I decided I hadn't heard the sounds of laughter behind me, and hoped my warm cheeks weren't obvious.

Back at my apartment I mentally patted myself on the back for remembering to take the shop tags off the babydoll and thong. The thong's string was bad enough, but having the price-tag up between my ass cheeks as well? No, thank you.

Then I had to get dressed in this stuff. I mentally cursed my cock as it began to get erect even before I'd stepped into the thong and slid up my legs. In fact I almost couldn't get my erection into it and reckoned the size I'd got was slightly too small as I had to yank the string up between my ass cheeks to give me enough room to stick my dick into the pink satin at the front. Even then it looked like some weird umbrella sticking out of the front of me. Thankfully the babydoll was a lot easier, but again, slightly smaller than the one I'd torn to pieces.

I felt a bit better putting my jeans and sweatshirt on as they hid the frilly pinkness. It strangely felt like I wasn't wearing anything underneath them. I put my trainers on and headed next door, managing to knock on the stroke of eight.

This time the door opened immediately.

She wore a knee-length shiny black leather skirt and matching black corset. The tops of her gorgeous breasts were straining to escape over the top. Dark nylons covered her legs, with shiny black heels on her feet. She'd slicked her hair back so that it was tight against her head and fell straight down to her shoulders. She looked incredibly hot. My dick especially liked the sight and immediately began trying to get to her. But why was she dressed like this?

She opened the door and I stepped through, basking in her scent.

"Hello, Sissy," she said, closing the door behind her.

"I'm not a sissy."

Then my heart stopped as a door opened and another beautiful girl came out and saw me. Her blond hair was cut short and framed her beautiful face. She wore a snake-print PVC miniskirt, matching bandeau over her taut breasts, and white calf-high stiletto boots. My dick jerked in welcome at seeing her.

"This is the sissy, Jen?" she said. "He's just in time."

"I'm not a sissy," I automatically said, then added, "And in time for what?"

"Sissy's in denial, Stace. You all set up in there?"

"Yeah."

"Come on," Jen turned to me.

"Where?"

"My bedroom. Isn't that where you want to go?"

I felt my cheeks heat up, then heard Stace laughing at me. "So sweet! He's a keeper, Jen. Watch out for your bras and panties though."

"I'm not–"

Stace interrupted, "Yeah, yeah. Heard it. Got bored the first time."

"Move," Jen said.

Almost reluctantly I followed both gorgeous girls into the bedroom.

A blue satin throw covered the single bed which had a table at its foot, with a laptop and a video camera on it pointing towards the bed. A bright light on a tall stand shone directly onto the bed leaving the rest of the room in darkness. What the fuck was going on?

The laptop screen showed the vacant bed. Stace walked behind the laptop and picked the video camera up while Jen went and sat on the bed, crossing her gorgeous legs.

"Ready?" she asked Stace.

"Just a sec."

What the hell?

"Ok."

Jen turned to me, "Show me what you're wearing."

From the corner of my eye I could make out Stace moving the camera over my body, with the picture displayed on the laptop screen.

"What the fuck is going on?"

"Not his head, Stace, he's not got his make-up or wig on."

"Right."

"So, a bit of background, Stace and me were looking to expand our adult only Youtube channel. But we didn't know what to add to it. But when I told her about finding you wearing my thong? Well, it kinda clicked into place and we've decided to see how catering for sissies goes."

"I'm not—"

She interrupted me, "Yeah, of course not. Anyway Stacey and I have had a good laugh at seeing you cum in my thong, and we thought other sissies—"

"I'm–"

"Give it a fucking break, Sissy," interrupted Stacey.

Oh god. I thought this couldn't get any worse. But now I was going to be the star in a fucking sissy Youtube channel.

"Show us the lingerie you're wearing, Sissy."

I hesitated, considering my options. What few of them there were.

Jen seemed to have read my thoughts as she said, "I've been doing some research."

I didn't answer, already fearing what she was going to say.

"And I know who your boss is, and their boss, and guess what?"

"What?" I carefully said.

"I know their boss as well. And, even better, I know their email addresses. So, unless you want them to see you cumming in a pink satin thong while wearing a frilly babydoll you'll show us what lingerie you're wearing. Trainers, jeans, top. Now, Sissy!"

I had no choice but to do as she said. Even I didn't know who my boss's boss's boss was, but reckoned they could do without seeing me doing that.

I pulled my sweatshirt up to show the frilly pink babydoll and then lowered my jeans slightly so she could see the top of the pink thong.

Jen looked confused at something, "Those aren't the ones I gave you?"

"Um, no. Something happened to them."

She smiled, "So you went and bought some more lingerie for yourself. Did you try any sexy panties on?"

"Maybe some lacy bras?" Stacey added, unhelpfully.

"Slutty garter belts?"

"Was that humiliating enough for you, Sissy?" asked Stacey. "Sissies love being humiliated, Jen. Really gets them off."

"We'll have to see what we can do about that then," she smiled at Stacey.

I ignored them and quickly undressed. My jeans and top lay on the floor next to my trainers. My dick, like some sort of Judas, pointed towards Jen, a dark patch of precum already showing through the pink satin thong.

"Sissy's really into you, Jen," Stacey laughed, focusing on it with the camera. "Aww, you look so cute. We've got a special present for you, Sissy."

I didn't answer.

Stacey picked up a box hidden by the laptop on the table and threw it on the bed next to Jen. Who in turn threw it to me. Reflexively I caught it.

"Stockings, put them on," Jen said.

"What?"

"Put them on."

Would this never stop?

I opened the box and took them out. I'd never handled stockings before and didn't have a clue what to do with them.

Seeing this she sighed and said, "Take one, roll it up your arm, take it off and feed it onto your foot, then slide it up your leg. Then repeat."

"Hey, Jen. I think we'll call this one, 'Novice Sissy'."

Jen laughed.

In the darker area of the desk I saw something shiny on the table that had been hidden under the box of stockings.

Somehow I managed to slide the stocking up my left leg. The lace top gripped my upper thigh, and my dick showed its appreciation of putting it on.

"Be faster with the right one."

I grunted at her.

"Your dick looks like it's ready to cum, Sissy," said Stacey.

I hoped it wouldn't as I didn't want yet more video of me cumming while wearing lingerie. Having some idea of how to put stockings on I was a shade faster with my right leg.

I stood in front of Jen, her sexy legs still crossed, wearing a frilly pink babydoll, a pink satin thong wet with my precum, and black lace-top hold-up stockings on my legs. I glanced at the laptop screen and quickly looked away.

"Good, Sissy. Don't worry, they'll be the first of many you'll wear. We've another treat for you," Jen said.

What the fuck now?

"I now want you to take your thong off. You know, the one you bought specially from a shop's lingerie department, and are currently getting wet with your precum?"

Ignoring the question I managed to extricate my erection from the wet thong and pull the string out from between my ass cheeks, then slid them down my stockings. Thrills went through me at the feeling.

"I can see your cock liked that," Jen said.

"Sissy's dripping precum, Jen! Disgusting!" Stacey smiled.

I took it off and held it away from me, like it had some sort of plague virus stuck to it.

"You bought it, put it on your other clothes."

I dropped it on my jeans.

Jen uncrossed her legs with a sensuous *shushing* sound, then leant over, showing me her gorgeous cleavage, picked up the shiny thing off the table and brought it into the brighter light. She opened it out and I saw it was a pair of pink satin panties with white lace trim.

They laughed at seeing my dick stand even more to attention.

Jen smiled. "I just knew you'd like them, Sissy. Put them on. We want to watch you jerk off in them."

"Yeah, it'll really go down well with the viewers."

I didn't like the sound of that. I closed my eyes, wishing it was all a nasty strange dream. I opened them again and saw my erect dick on the laptop screen, the end of it shiny with precum that was on the verge of dribbling down my cock. No, it wasn't a dream. It was a nightmare.

Jen threw the panties over to me. I caught them and took a deep breath before stepping into them. Thrills ran through me as I slid the smooth cool satin up my stockinged legs.

They felt wonderfully soft against my balls and erection.

"Jerk off for us, Sissy," Jen whispered. "Cum in your first pair of panties."

I gripped my cock through the pink satin and began to slowly rub it up and down.

"OMG!" Stacey excitedly whispered at the sight.

With how hot and sexy they both looked I knew it wouldn't be long before I came.

"Say it, Sissy. Tell me you're a sissy," Jen said.

"I'm not a sissy."

"You're going to cum in pink satin panties wearing a frilly babydoll and stockings. Everyone who sees this will know you're a sissy. Say it."

"I'm not a sissy."

"We're going to make you wear sexy dresses and short slutty skirts. Say it."

"I'm not a sissy."

"We're going to feminize you and make you into a pretty cocksucking cumslut. Say it."

I'd gradually been climbing the wall to an orgasm and now I was at the top. My stockinged legs trembled and I gasped as the orgasm crashed into me. My dick jerked and jerked again, firing my hot sperm into the satin panties. I felt its wetness against my hand gripping my jerking cock.

"Say it!"

"I'm a sissy!"

They burst out laughing as I stood in front of them in my lingerie and warm, wet panties. Humiliation washed over me even as I shot more and more of my load into the pink satin.

"Finished Sissy?" asked Jen.

"Yes," I whispered, horrified at what I'd just done.

"Jen?" said Stacey, as if reminding her of something.

"Yeah. Stacey and I need to set rules for you, Sissy."

What?

"You will address us as Mistress."

What?

"I am Mistress Jenny, and she is Mistress Stacey. You may go now, Sissy."

An even nastier surprise

The next day at work my blood pressure must have been all over the place – spiking with each email arrival and falling as I saw it didn't have a video attachment. How many people would have seen the video of me cumming? I hoped very very few. And that none of them could make out it was me.

Cassidy kept giving me strange looks, probably wondering what I'd done with the babydoll and thong she'd reserved for me. No way was I going to tell her. I was a nervous wreck by the time I'd finished for the day.

On the way home I visited a deli and got something for dinner.

Arriving home I carefully opened my door and peered round it to check for a note.

Nothing.

I looked over my shoulder at my neighbour's door. It was closed.

What was she up to? Or maybe she was out somewhere, tormenting another helpless male?

I breathed a sigh of relief and entered, closing the door firmly behind me.

Putting my dinner in the kitchen I went and checked the satin panties I'd washed with some shower gel last night, then stuck them on a radiator to dry. I hadn't torn them or the baby doll or stockings to shreds as I couldn't face having to buy any more replacements.

They were dry, which was pretty much a no-brainer as they'd had all day to do so. I took them into the bedroom and stopped. Something was different. Everything looked the same, but something was making the hairs on the back of my neck stand up. Still holding the panties I prowled round my bed. I was pretty sure everything was as I'd left it that morning, but why did something feel wrong?

The air! There was a very faint strange scent in the air! Someone had been in here while I'd been out. My heart fell - I could guess who. But what had she done? Just looked around? And how did she get in?

I carefully lifted the corner of my duvet up and peered underneath.

Deadly black scorpions failed to make an appearance.

Just to be sure I took the whole thing off. No, nothing.

I dropped the dry pink satin panties on the bed and continued my search.

Video cameras to film me?

I checked behind the vintage Star Wars film posters I'd decorated the room with.

Nothing.

The small glass vase from my mother was camera free.

Maybe my wardrobe, or chest of drawers, or bedside cabinets?

I approached my wardrobe like it was going to jump me. Sidling up to it I grabbed the door handle and yanked it open. My suits looked at me like I was losing it. I rummaged around inside looking for anything out of place. Nothing was.

Ok. I'd try the drawers where I kept my smaller stuff next.

The top drawer still held pens and old batteries and the receipts and bank statements I'd not bothered getting rid of yet.

My sock drawer was next. Yes, I had a drawer dedicated to my socks, what of it? I happen to like wearing socks, thank you very much.

They were all there.

I pulled out the drawer that I used for my boxers and multi-coloured panties exploded out and onto the floor. I sat back on the bed in surprise. She'd been in my apartment, in my bedroom, and in the drawer I used for my boxers to stick a load of female panties in it!

There was no way I was going to have panties in my boxers drawer! I pulled them out and threw them on the floor until the drawer was empty. The only male underwear I had was what I currently wore! Why the hell would she do that?

The scent I'd noticed earlier was now quite noticeable and somehow triggered the primal part of my brain. I picked a pair of red lacy panties up and sniffed them. They had a musky scent that definitely meant something to my dick. She'd worn them.

I caught sight of a note at the bottom of the drawer. With my heart sinking I reached in and took it out. Sitting back on my bed I opened it.

She was not going to stop.

~*~

All through the evening and night I wondered what I could do. I had to keep doing as she said or my life wouldn't be worth living. But should I wear panties to work? I had to try and ignore my dick thinking it would be a great idea. What could she do if I didn't? I wasn't too sure about going commando and not wearing any underwear, but what if I bought some boxers and changed into them in the gents at work and then changed back into panties after work? It would be a pain in the neck, but would provide me with a bit of a breather from the worry of being discovered wearing female panties at work.

I mean how would she know?

Having a plan seemed to work as I didn't remember falling asleep until my alarm beeped me awake in the morning.

I'd just finished my breakfast and was still in my warm fluffy dressing gown when my phone vibrated on the breakfast bar next to me.

Who would be calling at this hour?

I picked it up and accepted the call. I wish I hadn't.

Jen looked at me, her hair loose, and gorgeous. "Show me," she said.

"What?"

"Show me the panties you'll be wearing today."

Oh fuck. What could I say?

"I… um, haven't decided yet."

"Then I, as your Mistress, will decide for you. Show me the drawer."

My stomach fell as I stood up and took my phone, and Mistress Jenny, into the bedroom. So this was how she was going to make sure I wore panties all day. My plan was blown.

I knelt down in front of the drawer, pulled it open and turned the phone so she could see what was in the drawer.

"Hmm, those, the black satin ones."

I took them out.

"I remember getting them really wet while thinking about being fucked by a large cock. I think I rubbed my clit through them. By now they should be crispy with my dried pussy juice. You'll love them, Sissy."

I could smell her muskiness on them and wondered what would happen on my commute to and from work, and what might happen in work if someone smelt them on me.

"Don't worry, Sissy, I'll check you're still wearing them throughout the day. And tonight Stace and I have got something special planned for Channel Sissy."

~*~

Throughout my commute I wondered when she'd call me to check I still wore the slightly too small black satin panties that were still musky with her scent. Also what I'd have to do to show her I still wore them. I'd turned the sound off on my phone so would only know she called when my phone vibrated.

I got a few strange looks from people standing next to me on the crowded subway, but ignored them. I mean how could *I* be the one smelling of dried musky pussy juice?

I took a deep breath emerging from the subway at my last stop. Now all I had to do was survive work. But what then awaited me in the evening? What had those two bitches got planned for me on Channel Sissy?

Not that I was one, of course.

But then a thought hit me – what if someone from work had watched what I did last night? Would they realise it was me? I reckoned it wasn't a mainstream Youtube channel. Jen, or Mistress Jenny, did say not to film my face as I'd not got any make… Oh, shit, Make-up. They were going to make me up tonight.

They also said they'd just started the channel. But the internet is forever. Maybe someone would stumble across the video in the future? Maybe I'd be dead by then? I could but hope.

I was just about to sit down at my desk when my phone vibrated in my trousers. I jerked upright with a cry like my ass had just been tazered.

At the next desk to mine Cassidy also jumped in surprise and glared at me, "What the fuck is wrong with you?" she hissed.

"Just need… just need to visit… Sorry." I hurried off with my phone still vibrating, sending thrills to my dick.

What the fuck was I going to do? Then it hit me – the gents.

Finally safe in a stall I answered the call. Jen mouthed something at me. I whispered, "I've turned the sound down."

She turned away and did something out of shot, then turned back holding up a piece of paper with 'Show me' written and underlined on it.

I quickly unzipped my trousers and aimed the phone at my black satin-covered crotch.

I looked back at her and saw she'd written on a new piece of paper 'Good Sissy' with a little heart next to it. Then she hung up.

Back at my desk I had to do something about the musky scent coming from my crotch so kept my little desk fan on and had far too many cups of coffee, making sure to spill a few on my desk, to try and mask the smell. I reckoned by now Cassidy had made a completely new weirdo-meter just for me.

I managed to make it through work without any mishaps, then went home. I dreaded my phone going off while I was on the subway

~*~

The subway was crowded and I stood wedged between strangers looking at their phones, my backpack between my feet and holding a flexible handle attached to the ceiling. I'd already noticed the twitchy noses of those close to me as the musky scent of the panties slowly gained their attention.

I counted the stops still to go before I could get off, wishing I was already home and that someone had invented a teleportation device so I could be there instantly and wouldn't have to smell anyone's overly powerful aftershave.

She'd not got me on the morning commute, but–

I jerked in surprise as my phone vibrated.

I shouldn't have thought about it! I'd jinxed myself!

The people close to me glared as I bumped against them, disturbing their phone gazing.

Carefully I reached into my pocket and took my phone out. It was her. What the fuck was I going to do?!

I answered the call and tried to give her a view of the people well inside my personal space, and hence the impossibility of showing her the panties, as well as hiding the screen from those around me.

She didn't seem impressed and held up the paper with 'Show me' written on it.

How the hell was I going to show her the panties I wore? I mean I'd probably be in danger of some indecency law. Was there one now? Maybe to do with horses? Couldn't remember.

She shook the paper at me and I tried my best to hide the screen from anyone looking over my shoulder.

What could I do?

No way was I going to lower my trousers, even if that was possible on a moving subway train without falling over and someone attacking me for being a pervert.

Shitshitshitshit!

Fuck it. I did the only thing I could do – I stuck my phone down my trousers so she could try and see the panties in the light from the phone.

I caught the surprised look of the people standing close to me and ignored them, like it was something utterly normal, then brought my phone out. Looking at the screen I caught sight of the 'Good Sissy' piece of paper before I quickly ended the call.

~*~

I made it through the door of my apartment and collapsed, feeling like I'd just mentally run a marathon. What would I have done if she'd rung while I was on the street? Found a convenient dark alleyway? Got into a Superman-free phone box and smashed the overhead light and then flashed the panties I wore at my phone?

Anyway, nothing good. And, even better, I was safe. Or at least safe-ish. And not arrested for indecent behaviour, unless someone decided to report a strange man with a strange smell on the subway. Yeah, like the cops would look into that.

I cried out in surprise as my phone vibrated yet again.

Closing my eyes I sighed deeply before taking it out and answering it.

The phone was still on silent so I only saw Mistress Jenny move her mouth. I turned the sound up and heard, "-for you next door, Sissy."

"What? I've just got in and missed the first part."

She rolled her eyes and said, "We've got a present for you next door, Sissy."

"Oh."

"So you'll be here in the next minute."

"Can't I get changed first?"

She smiled a smile that didn't reach her eyes. "You can get changed over here, Sissy."

She hung up.

I dragged myself up off the floor and into the kitchen where I grabbed a drink of orange juice, then headed next door.

Preparation

A vision in red satin opened the door. The red satin robe she wore was edged with black lace and only went down to her mid-thigh. It barely hid her gorgeous breasts that were pushed up by a red satin corset. The robe wasn't tightly tied by the red satin belt and fell open as I entered, and I saw she wore matching red panties, a red garter belt, black stockings, and shiny red stilettos.

My dick forced itself against the musky black satin panties I wore under my trousers. I caught a sniff of the perfume she wore and knew I was lost.

Closing the door behind me she said, "Undress, Sissy."

"Yeah."

She stalked in front of me, her dark hair loose, her beautiful eyes blazing with anger and slapped my face.

My left cheek burned, "What?!" I held my cooler hand against it ready to stop another slap.

She hissed angrily, "You do not disrespect me! You will address me as Mistress Jenny. I told you yesterday. or have you already forgotten the 'or else'?"

The fire in my cheek lessened and I reluctantly said, "No... No, Mistress Jenny."

"Good. Undress, Sissy."

"Yes, Mistress Jenny."

I used one shoe to slip the other shoe off, then repeated it. Then slowly took my suit jacket off and dropped it on the floor.

Her stilettos clicked on the hard floor as she headed over to one of the leather chairs which was turned away from me, where a suit carrier lay draped over the back.

She sat on the chair's arm and crossed her legs to watch me undress. My trousers joined the jacket and I began to unbutton my shirt.

She reached over, unconcernedly letting the red satin robe fall open, and unzipped the suit carrier. What the hell was in it?

"What's a sissy's favourite outfit?" she asked.

My shirt fell to the floor and I stood in front of her wearing the black satin panties, and socks. "As I'm not a sissy I don't know." Before quickly adding, "Mistress Jenny."

She opened the suit carrier and shiny black satin and white lace burst forth.

"A French maid. A sexy French maid, just begging to please their mistress. Or master."

My first thought was that she'd look so hot in that! My dick hardened even more, smearing my precum against the musky black satin panties I wore.

And then…

Wait.

Wait a second.

I was going to wear it.

"Socks," she instructed.

"Yes, Mistress Jenny," I quietly said.

"Come over here and sit down while I do your make-up. Leave your panties on for a moment, I don't want your precum getting on my chair."

I whispered, "Yes, Mistress Jenny."

"I'll make you look so pretty!"

"Yes, Mistress Jenny."

I walked over and sat down in the vacant chair, the leather cold against my bare skin and panty-covered ass.

In the seat of the one she sat on was a tray containing all sorts of make-up items - lipsticks, small brushes, round plastic containers. Items I'd never really cared much about, but now knew they'd be used on me. Something that resembled a hairy blond cat also lay there. For a moment I wondered what it was. And then it hit me – it was a wig.

Mistress Jenny picked up the make-up tray and came over to sit on the arm of the chair I sat in. The fragrance she wore tightening its grip around my soul.

"Hold this," she said, giving me the tray of make-up

"Yes, Mistress Jenny."

"Look up at me and close your eyes, Sissy,"

"Yes, Mistress Jenny."

I did so and felt her lift items off the tray and then stuff being wiped on me, and brushed on me, and stuck to my eyelids, and finally smeared over my lips making them feel like I needed a napkin to wipe sticky sauce off.

I could only imagine how stupid I looked. Like some sort of really bad clown.

The tray was lifted out of my hands and I felt and heard her move to the other chair.

She came back and I flinched as she brushed my hair back. Then something tight was placed on my head, gripping my short hair. The strange feeling of hair different to my own brushing against my ears sent shivers down my back.

Something was stuck on top and pinned to the wig I wore.

"Open your eyes."

"Yes, Mistress Jenny," I said feeling my strangely greasy lips move.

I did so and felt the slight weight of whatever she'd stuck to my eyelids. She was examining my face intently. I lost myself in her eyes.

"That'll do," she said, satisfied with her work. Standing up she added, "Take your panties off and put the lingerie and outfit on."

"Yes, Mistress Jenny."

She walked away towards the bedroom while I looked at the way her tight ass moved in the red satin robe she wore.

I got up and took the panties off while she opened the door slightly and peered round. I heard muffled laughter that I guessed was from Mistress Stacey. But then my blood froze at hearing a male's deeper laughter.

What were they going to make me do?

She went into the room leaving me to dress myself as a French maid. I walked over to the suit carrier, making sure to avoid looking at myself in the mirrors. Taking out the French maid uniform I saw white satin lingerie, a box of black fishnet stockings, and shiny black heels to go with it. I lay the uniform on the chair's armrest and started changing.

~*~

Some sixth sense told me someone was looking at me. I turned round and saw Stacey and Jenny looking at me from the open bedroom door, phones in their hands taking pictures of me. This evening Stacey wore tight shiny black leggings and a red leopard-pattern bandeau.

"He looks so slutty!" said Stacey. "Especially with those fishnets! Good job, Jen."

"Thanks, Hun. You can tell he's a sissy, just look at his erection!"

Underneath my make-up my cheeks burned. I was well aware of my erection as I'd had trouble getting it into the white satin thong as well as pulling the black satin and lace uniform up over it. I could already feel my precum smearing against the smooth thong material.

But I wasn't a sissy!

I reached round my back and managed to find the uniform's zip. Carefully, not wanting to dislocate anything, I zipped myself into the outfit they wanted me to wear. It felt strange – tight around my torso and upper body, and non-existent around my legs. I'd only seen women wear French maid uniforms before and they looked hot. But me? I probably looked stupid.

Jen and Stacey looked at each other, glee clear in their faces. I adjusted the short frilly French maid uniform and got ready to put the shiny black stilettos on.

"We've got another surprise for you, Sissy," said Jen.

81

I was already feeling humiliated enough and didn't want to have even more added to it.

"When you've put the shoes on, come over here," Stacey said.

Holding the back of the chair for balance I slid my right foot into the stiletto. It fitted but it felt like I was having to balance on tip-toe. I slid my left foot into the other one, feeling my centre of gravity shift.

"Looking good, Sissy," said Jen. "Now come over here."

Very slowly, and with my arms held out to the sides for balance I took small steps towards them. They burst out laughing at me, but I didn't want to fall over and break my ankles.

They glanced at each other again and Stacey disappeared into the room.

Muffled voices came to me. Who was in there with Stacey? Hopefully no-one I knew. But what would they want me to do?

Channel Sissy

Mistress Jenny's phone filmed me walking over to her in the short frilly French maid uniform and high stiletto shoes they wanted me to wear. She had one hand behind her back, but at the moment all I could concentrate on was not falling over.

"Ok, Stace?" she asked over her shoulder.

"Ready in here."

"Get ready to start filming."

"'kay."

Fear took hold of me and I quietly asked, "What's going to happen, Mistress Jenny?"

She looked at me, "A sissy's dream is going to come true."

"Bu–"

"Don't care what you think, Sissy," she interrupted. "You're going to make us money."

She looked at me, letting her words sink in. I was just a plaything for them. My humiliation was going to make them money and that's all they cared about.

"Stand still."

I did so, glad to be only wobbling in place and not trying to walk in the high stiletto heels.

She walked round behind me and grabbed my left arm, yanking it behind me.

"What?!" I cried out, desperately trying not to fall over.

Something cold was clicked round my wrist. Then my right arm was grabbed and pulled back as well. Another sharp click and I realised I couldn't bring my arms back round - I'd been handcuffed.

"No!"

Slap!

"Sissy will shut the fuck up!" she hissed angrily at me.

My right cheek burned, but this time not with humiliation.

She moved to stand in front of me and brought something else out from behind her back – a long silvery-metal chain with a pink leather collar, "Hold still."

I stood still or I'd probably break my ankles.

She unbuckled the collar and fed the pink leather around my neck, then buckled it back up. "How tight should I make it, Sissy?" she smiled.

Her hand found its way underneath the short black satin skirt and gripped my erection. "Hmm, I could tell you liked a dominant woman forcing you to wear sexy female clothes."

But I wasn't a sissy!

I stayed silent.

She turned and called out, "Sissy's ready, Stace. You ready?"

"Yeah. Starting to film now."

She turned back to me and gave me an evil smile. Then suddenly jerked the leash.

"Ow!" I cried out, stumbling towards her in the high stilettos.

"It's showtime, Sissy."

She unbelted her red satin robe, letting it fall open, then turned to walk towards the bedroom door with me unwillingly having to follow.

Mistress Stacey stood holding the camera next to the table, and on the laptop screen I saw a leashed French maid with short blond hair being brought into the room by a beautiful lady wearing sexy red lingerie.

And then I caught sight of the bed.

A naked muscular man lay on the white satin cover, his cock was limp but still longer than mine and lay on top of his thigh. He was creamy coffee-coloured and had short dark hair, and a knowing smile.

Stacey walked around us with the camera, getting me from all angles. Even up the short French maid uniform skirt to show the white satin thong barely holding my cock and balls.

"I'm feeling horny, Sissy, and need a hard cock to fuck me. As my sissy French maid your task is to serve me, so I want you to make him hard for me," Jen said in a strangely loud voice. Then I realised she was playing for the camera.

But she meant it about me having to suck a cock.

Oh shit.

I stood there, unwilling to move.

The leash was jerked down and I was only just able to stop myself falling flat on my face. The black fishnet stockings failed to provide any protection as my knees hit the floor.

"Ow!"

I felt Jen lift my shirt frilly skirt up and then–

Slap!

"Ow!"

This time my ass cheek was the one to feel the burn.

"Bad, Sissy! What do you say?"

What?

Slap!

"Ow!"

Oh, yeah. "Sorry, Mistress Jenny."

"Better. For your bad behaviour I'll increase the size of your butt plug tonight."

What the fuck?!

"Yes, Mistress Jenny."

She pulled the leash, forcing me to walk on my knees towards the guy on the bed or I'd fall flat on the floor.

He slid his toned body up into a sitting position, his long dark cock hanging down over the white satin edge of the bed.

I was going to do this?

I was going to take another man's penis in my mouth?

And suck on it to make it hard?

Was there anything I could do to stop it?

Didn't seem like it.

A strange feeling fluttered around in my stomach and sent tingles to my balls.

But I wasn't a sissy!

"I know you sissies love sucking cocks, but you mustn't swallow his sperm as I want him to fuck me."

Stacey moved in closer with the camera.

Jen twisted the metal chain leash around her hand and pulled my head nearer to the guy's dick. With my hands cuffed behind me I had to shuffle forwards on my knees.

"Take it in your mouth, Sissy. Make it hard for your mistress," Jen purred. "Maybe I'll give you a treat after he's fucked me."

The guy moved his muscular legs wider apart so as to give both me and the camera room. I kept my long lashes down, not wanting to look up into his face and see what pleasure I was going to give another man.

Jen's hand came into view and picked his cock up. It looked like a long, thick floppy sausage.

"Open wide, Sissy."

I closed my eyes and opened my mouth. Something warm and large and musky was placed in my mouth, resting heavily on my tongue. I had another man's cock in my mouth! Something I'd never ever thought of doing. More tingles went through me, and I could feel my own dick stiffen more.

"Now suck his cock, Sissy. Rub your soft glossy lips along its length," Jen whispered.

But I didn't want to.

She must have seen my hesitation as-

Slap!

I jerked forwards away from the slap on my ass but couldn't cry out as I'd taken more of the long cock in.

"I said suck it!"

I remembered the many cock-sucking videos I'd watched over the years and closed my lips around it's girth. It felt enormous! Did they all feel as large as this one? Those girls needed more credit for what they did!

Slowly Jen used the leash to force my head to move back and forth along the soft cock, my lips rubbing against it. I had to try to balance on my knees or I'd fall face first into his groin and take him balls-deep. Quite quickly I felt his dick begin to harden and straighten up.

Stacey's camera got near to my face, getting close-ups of a sissy French maid sucking a large cock. The thought made me conscious of my own dick now pushing against the white satin of my thong.

"Moan, Sissy. Show us how much you're enjoying it. Or I'll spank you again."

Jen moved my head to take more and more of the cock in, getting it wetter and wetter with my saliva, until I began to feel the gag reflex kick in.

I began to moan – I didn't want to be spanked again.

"Told you Sissy was a natural cock-sucker," Jen said to Stacey. "Let's see how he's done for his first time."

I was pulled off the cock, grateful I could finally close my mouth.

"Reckon that's hard enough, Stacey?" asked Jen.

"Nearly. Looks like sissy's really getting into it."

I jerked at the feeling of her touching my own dick and balls.

"Get him to lick the tip," she added.

"You heard her, Sissy. Lick the tip. See if you can taste any pre-cum."

Again my mouth was pulled closer to the guy's shiny wet stiff erection. I stuck the tip of my tongue out and touched it to the tip of his cock. I could taste salt. My stomach nearly rebelled with the knowledge that this was another man's sperm. But my dick didn't.

"Well, Sissy?"

"Yes, Mistress, I can taste his pre-cum."

"Good."

Stacey and her camera moved around to the front.

With a metallic rattle of the leash's chain Jen unwound it from her hand, letting me kneel back, then stepped in front of me showing the back of her black stockings, and straddled the guy's legs with her knees on the bed. From my low vantage point I saw her pull the gusset of her red panties to one side and then slowly lower herself onto the guy's erect cock.

She gave a deep groan as it slowly went deeper and deeper into her wet cunt.

I couldn't do anything as she still had hold of the leash. She was going to fuck the guy with me on my knees watching?

"Ohhh," she groaned. "Sissy's made it so wet."

Her leg muscles tensed and she slowly lifted up off it, then lowered herself down, taking it even deeper. The guy groaned enjoying her hot pussy surrounding his hard cock.

"God, Stace, this is good cock," she managed to whisper, lifting up again.

Slowly she began to speed up, her musky scent getting stronger.

"Lick his balls, Sissy," Stacey ordered.

I saw them hanging over the side of the white satin bed like some weird brown fruit. The camera appeared to my side and I shuffled on my knees closer to them. I'd already taken his cock into my mouth, this was less worse than that.

Above my head Mistress Jenny's gorgeous ass moved up and down as she took pleasure in riding the guy's erection.

I closed my eyes and stuck my tongue out smelling the combined musk of the two of them. The tip of my tongue touched something and I felt him jerk.

"Good sissy," said Stacey. "Lick them until I tell you to suck them."

"Yes, Mistress Stacey."

Still with my eyes closed I licked his sac, pushing it against the white satin sheet, feeling his hard balls move around inside, and hearing him groan. Whether that was from me or Mistress Jenny's wet cunt I didn't know.

"Now suck them, Sissy."

I opened my mouth wider and took his sac in. This time I knew I was the one to make him groan with pleasure. My own erection was now pushing against the thong so much that the string was slowly climbing up between my cheeks.

But I wasn't a sissy!

"That's so good," the guy moaned, as I used my tongue to bounce his balls around in my mouth. The video camera caught the sight in all its gory glory.

Mistress Jenny's moans were getting louder and quicker. I guessed she was close to orgasming. What would happen then?

"Stace!" she almost screamed. The camera moved from me and I guessed it was now catching Mistress Jenny's orgasm.

Her ass stopped moving above me and I saw her leg muscles tighten as her orgasm hit.

"Omygodohmygodohmygod!" she screamed aloud.

The guy's balls jerked in my mouth and I knew he was cumming as well.

"HOOO!" he cried, his legs spasming, as he fired his cum again and again into Mistress Jenny's hot cunt.

Slowly his ejaculations decreased and Mistress Jenny caught her breath as she slowly moved her ass up releasing his cock. I saw something white begin to drip down from her cunt and flow down his erection. She took a deep breath like she'd not been able to breathe for the last minute and rolled off him, lying exhausted by his side. The guy's still erect cock was covered with a mixture of his glistening white cum and her pussy juice. She lay to the side breathing heavily, slowly getting her breath back.

"Let his balls go, Sissy," she managed to gasp.

I did so, and knelt back, seeing Mistress Jenny's face sweaty from her recent exertions.

"Time for the money shot, Jen," Mistress Stacey said.

What did she mean by that?

Mistress Jenny moved her right leg up and over the guy's torso, giving me a full view of her cum-leaking pussy.

Mistress Stacey moved behind me and, much to my surprise, released me from the handcuffs. My arms sprang round to my front and I put my hands down on the floor for long-needed support.

"Want to know your treat, Sissy?" asked Stacey.

Well, not really.

"We're going to let you cum."

"But only after you've cleaned my pussy, and then his cock, first," Mistress Jenny added.

Almost without conscious thought my right hand reached between my legs and underneath my frilly French maid skirt to grasp my own hard erection through the white satin thong.

Was I really going to do this?

I moved round the guy's legs towards Mistress Jenny's cum-leaking pussy.

Was I a sissy?

Did I secretly enjoy the humiliation of a beautiful woman forcing me to wear sexy female clothes and sucking a man's cock and then swallowing his sperm?

Mistress Stacey's camera captured every moment of me licking the hot salty semen from Mistress Jenny's cunt and swallowing it down.

I couldn't remember having such a hard erection for such a long time before this.

After her cunt was spotless I moved onto the guy's messy cock, but before I'd fully cleaned it of his sperm my excitement made me cum, shooting my own semen into the white satin thong where it dripped onto the floor. Mistress Stacey didn't seem to mind and caught it all on video.

I knew I'd be punished and be made to clean it up, probably with my tongue, but the idea sent excited thrills through me.

"Don't worry, Sissy, next time we'll let him fuck you," said Mistress Stacey.

Was I a sissy?

I guess so.

***

Ugly Duckling – 3

Friday Night 2: Trixie

Friday Night 3: Rochelle

Sissy Dreams: Being Kellie

Sissy Dreams: Sally's Evening Out

Office Sissy: The Form

Office Sissy: Personal Assistant

Mistress Dyke's Fembot Factory

Sissy Dreams: A Prissy Sissy Dream

Sissy Dreams: The New Maid

Hazed by the Cheerleader Brat

Sissy Dreams: The First Time

Sissy Dreams: For Hire

College Girl Discipline

Ugly Duckling – 4

Office Sissy: Appraisal

Punished by my Mistress

Sissy Dreams: Chris & Chyna

For Hire: My First Time

Office Sissy: Company Policy

Sissy Dreams: Lost Vacation
(Ebook exclusive to Smashwords)

Sissy Dreams: A Very Prissy Sissy Day

Sissy Dreams: Sissy, Disciplined

Sissy Dreams: The New Job

Sissy Dreams: From Boyfriend to Girlfriend

Collections

Sissy Erotica Collection, Part One

Contains: Maid Charlotte and the Lesbian Television Presenters, Secretary Charlotte and the Eager Athlete, Maid Charlotte and the Other Maid, Glamour Charlotte and the Awards Night, Ugly Duckling – 1, Ugly Duckling - 2.

Sissy Erotica Collection, Part Two

Contains: Secretary Charlotte Makes a Sissy Maid, Maid Charlotte Tricks or Treats, Maid Charlotte Breaks the Ice, College Girl, Prostitute, Ugly Duckling – 3.

Sissy Erotica Collection, Part Three

Contains: Sally's T.o.t.m., Friday Night 1: Lexie, A Gift For You, Friday Night 2: Trixie, Night Out, Friday Night 3: Rochelle, and Being Kellie.

Sissy Erotica Collection, Part Four

Contains: A Prissy Sissy Dream, Mistress Dyke's Fembot Factory, Office Sissy: The Form, Office Sissy: Personal Assistant, The New Maid, and Hazed by the Cheerleader Brat.

Sissy Erotica Collection: Part Five

Contains: A Prissy Sissy Dream, Mistress Dyke's Fembot Factory, Office Sissy: The Form, Office Sissy: Personal Assistant, The New Maid, and Hazed by the Cheerleader Brat.

Sissy Erotica Collection: Part Six
Contains: Chris & Chyna, Office Sissy: Company Policy, Wing Girl, Trainee Sales Assistant, Sissy of the House: Burnt Toast, and For Hire: My First Time.

Sissy Erotica Collection, Part Seven
Contains: Bad Girls, Sissy of the House: Naughty College Girl, The Promise, Miss Kitty's, For Hire: The Favour, and Mistress Dyke's Evil Experiment.

Sissy Dreams: Collection 1
Contains: College Girl, Prostitute, and Sally's T.o.t.M.

Sissy Dreams: Collection 2
Contains: A Gift For You, Night Out, Being Kellie, and Sally's Evening Out.

Sissy Dreams: Collection 3
Contains: Office Sissy: The Form, and Personal Assistant, and Mistress Dyke's Fembot Factory.

Sissy Dreams: Collection 4
Contains: Sissy Dreams: a Prissy Sissy Dream, Sissy Dreams: The New Maid, and Hazed by the Cheerleader Brat.

Sissy Dreams: Collection 5
Contains: Sissy Dreams: The First Time, Sissy Dreams: For Hire, and College Girl Discipline.

Sissy Dreams: Collection 6
Contains: Ugly Duckling – 4, Office Sissy: Appraisal, and Punished by my Mistress.

Sissy Dreams: Collection 7
Contains: Sissy Dreams: Chris & Chyna, Office Sissy: Company Policy, and For Hire: My First Time.

Sissy Dreams: Collection 8

Contains: Wing Girl, Trainee Sales Assistant, Sissy of the House: Burnt Toast, and Sissy of the House: A Gift for Master.

Sissy Dreams: Collection 9

Contains: Sissy Dreams: Bad Girls, Sissy of the House: Maid for my Mistress, Sissy of the House: Naughty College Girl, and Sissy Dreams: The Promise

Sissy Dreams: Collection 10

Contains: Sissy Dreams: Miss Kitty's, For Hire: The Favour, and Mistress Dykes' Evil Experiment.

Sissy Dreams: Collection 11

Contains: Office Girls Revenge, A Prissy sissy Story, and Motel Sissy.

Sissy Dreams: Collection 12

Contains: One of the Girls, Motel Sissy – 2, and Channel Sissy.

Sissy Dreams: Collection 13

Contains: Sissies in Trouble, A very Prissy Sissy Day, and Sissy, Disciplined.

Ugly Duckling Collection 1

Contains: parts 1, 2, and 3 of Ugly Duckling.

Friday Night Collection One

Contains: Lexie, Trixie, and Rochelle.

Office Sissy Collection 1

Contains: The Form, Personal Assistant, and Appraisal.

Sissy of the House: Collection One

Contains: Burnt Toast, A Gift for Master, and Maid for my Mistress.

For Hire: Collection One

Contains: For Hire, For Hire: My First Time, and For Hire: The Favour.